ADIRONDACK FAIRY TALES II

Tell Me a Story

by Lettie Petrie
Illustrated by Beth Petrie

ADDITIONAL TITLES
BY THE AUTHOR

Adirondack Fairy Tales

The Erie Canal Series

Book One:
*Minnie the Mule
and the Erie Canal*

Coming Soon:
Book Two
A Baker's Dozen

Adirondack Fairy Tales II
Tell Me A Story

by Lettie A. Petrie
Copyright © 2002

Illustrated by Beth L. Petrie

Printed in the United States Of America
by Patterson Printing, Michigan

Library of Congress Cataloguing-in-Publication-Data

CIP applied for
ISBN 0-9711638-1-2

Published By
PETRIE PRESS
9 Card Avenue
Camden NY 13316

DEDICATION

*This book is for a new generation
of grandchildren, Andrew, Emily, Nicholas,
Noah, and all of those who will follow.
And it is written for children everywhere
who like to listen to stories, or read them.*

ADIRONDACK FAIRY TALES II

Tell Me a Story

INDEX

B. PETRIE
'02

ADIRONDACK FAIRY TALES II

SOLOMON

ONCE UPON A TIME there was a forest in the Adirondack Mountains where only a few humans were ever seen. There were great numbers of rabbits, raccoons, skunks and fox in this woodland. Chipmunks scampered around the clearings. Small birds twittered on low branches of the trees. Pheasants flew, and fat partridges hid in the thick brush, flying with a whir of wings when they were alarmed. The river running through this beautiful glade was home to glistening fish and fat bullfrogs, as well as ducks and geese. There were snakes and bugs and worms…and the ruler of this animal kingdom was a Great White Owl called Solomon.

In this forest there were good animals and there were hungry, selfish animals. Until Solomon became their ruler, small helpless creatures of the forest suffered when they were robbed of their food, or were driven from their dens.

Sometimes they were hurt when they defended their homes. From his perch high in the branches of a giant pine tree Solomon's sharp yellow eyes saw the bad things happen. Many times he flew to the rescue, spreading his big wings and screeching at the top of his lungs until the enemy retreated.

After years of living in fear, the peaceful animals decided to make Solomon their ruler. They learned to listen to him, and he taught them how to warn each other of danger. He helped them to drive the bad animals out of their kingdom.

There came a day that great trouble came to this beautiful forest. It was fall in the mountains. The ground was covered with bright, dry leaves that fell from the trees. A careless camper left his campfire burning when he left the woods and a breeze blew a spark into the leaves. They caught fire!

Solomon was asleep in the top of his favorite pine

tree. The fire had spread before the frightened cries of the animals in its path reached his ears. Quickly, he dropped to the lower branches of the tree, and his sharp eyes saw the danger. The fire was creeping across the banks of the river! Soon it would reach the trees! *We must warn the Forest Rangers!* He led them out of the glen, flying towards the village, and the animals followed, even though they were afraid of the humans who lived there. They trusted their leader. Soon they reached a cabin where people were packing their belongings into cars. When they saw the big white owl and all of the animals who followed him, they were afraid. *What is happening?*

Solomon circled above them. All of the birds who had followed circled with him, calling at the top of their lungs. Deer pawed the ground before they turned to run back to the glen, but they stopped to look back at the people.

"They want us to go with them!" A little girl shouted as she came out of her cabin. "I smell smoke!" She pointed to the forest behind them before running back to the cabin to call the Ranger's station. Fire engines raced to the glen as smoke rose, white and billowing. The Rangers showed the people how to pump water from the river and dig ditches around the fire.

Now that Solomon and the other animals knew help had come, they fled back into the woods, and the humans wondered how the animals knew they should come to warn them before the fire reached the trees. Only the animals of the forest knew that it was Solomon who had saved them.

B. PETRIE
02

FERDIE'S FABULOUS FIREFLY

HIGH IN THE Adirondack Mountains Ferdie frog lives under a lily pad at Buttermilk Falls. Ferdie was born a tadpole. While he was a tadpole he could live only in the water. His arms and legs grew slowly out of his body and he lost his long tail. He still remembers the day he finally grew his legs and became a frog. At last he could hop out of the water and move around on the sunny bank of his stream. He was happy!

Ferdie is handsome. He has big black eyes near the top of his head. His enormous mouth stretches from one side of his head to the other, so he always looks like he is smiling. His long, sticky tongue is hooked to the front of his mouth. He uses it to catch his food.

His long back legs bend in the middle so that he can jump a long way, and his short front arms catch him when he lands. His feet are webbed so that he can swim through the water. Ferdie can live under the water or on land. When he is in his stream, he breathes through his shiny green skin, and when he is on land, he sucks air into his mouth with his long tongue. When he climbs to the top of his lily pad he can watch for insects and listen for their buzzing noise.

Ferdie likes to eat flies. He thinks they are delicious. Late one afternoon, just as it was growing dark, Ferdie sat on his lily pad feeling very hungry. He looked at the dark water and he spied a *Big* fly. He flicked out his sticky tongue and the fly stuck to its middle! He closed his mouth, ready to enjoy his dinner. A bright light came on inside his mouth! He was so surprised that he did not swallow. He moved his tongue carefully. The light went out. *Now he could swallow his meal!* No…. there was that light again!

A little voice called, "Let me out! Let me out!"

Ferdie opened his mouth a tiny bit and said, "I am hungry. You are a fly. I am going to eat you." He closed his mouth firmly.

The light went on again. "Please! Let me go and I will find you lots of insects. I am only one fly. I am not a good meal for a big frog like you."

Ferdie didn't know if he should believe this little voice, but it was true that one fly was not a very good meal. "You will fly away if I let you out. Why should I believe you will bring me more insects to eat?"

"My name is Flame. I am not just a fly – I am a firefly. I will light my lamp and insects will follow me. You can eat them instead of me."

Ferdie thought about how hungry he was. "How do I know you will keep your promise?"

Flame said, "If you let me out, I promise to bring you a lot of insects every day."

Every day? He would like that! Ferdie decided to trust the firefly. "I am going to let you out, but if you do not bring me insects, I will eat every firefly I can find."

He opened his big mouth and Flame flew away. His light twinkled. Ferdie watched him disappear. His eyes blinked. *I am so dumb! That firefly will not bring me insects. He just wanted to get away.* His stomach growled because he was so hungry.

Suddenly, he saw a tiny light. *Could that be Flame?*

The light came closer, and Flame called, "Put out your tongue. Here comes your dinner!"

The little firefly swung away as Ferdie's tongue

caught a whole swarm of small black flies that were following Flame's light. Ferdie swallowed quickly. Those insects tasted wonderful …. much better than just one firefly!

Flame's light flickered as he flew around Ferdie. "I kept my promise. You have your reward for letting me go. Tomorrow I will bring you more insects if you promise not to eat me or my family."

"You are fabulous! I will never eat a firefly!" Freddie croaked.

Almost everyone knows that fireflies like to come out when it grows dark. Look carefully, and if Ferdie sees you, he will greet you with a big smile while he sings his croaking song.

ADIRONDACK FAIRY TALES II
Tell Me a
Story

LLOYD & LAVERN PARTNERS AGAINST CRIME

T HERE WAS A TIME that llamas lived only in the country of Peru. The people there rode them like ponies. They knew that llamas could go for long distances without getting tired, and that they were good hill climbers.

Not too many years ago some wise sheep farmers, who lived in the foothills of the Adirondack Mountains in our country, found a new use for these woolly animals. They learned that llamas would guard their flocks of sheep better than their sheep dogs did.

TELL ME A STORY 13

One farmer bought two llamas and named them Lloyd and Laverne. Their round, woolly bodies looked a little like their new friends, the sheep, but Lloyd and Laverne had long, powerful legs with sharp hooves. Their long necks and perky ears tilted forward, and they could see the farthest corners of their pasture. Their keen eyes and sharp noses told them when there was danger. Both of them were creamy white, like some of the sheep, and they had a brown patch on their backs that looked almost like a saddle.

Farmer Peters found that he could sell their wool to make sweaters, even though it was different than the wool of the sheep. Unlike the sheep, who seemed unaware of danger until it was too late to save themselves, Lloyd and Laverne were always alert.

One day a hungry coyote, who looked a little like a dog, and a little like a wolf, came creeping towards the herd. The llamas sensed his presence and their soft *"hum"* became a sharp *"hiss."* They were warning that sneaky coyote that it was not going to be easy for him to get a sheep for dinner.

Still, that evil coyote came slinking towards the sheep. He was hungry! Lloyd and Laverne's powerful legs sped across the pasture, and they hissed loudly. The coyote stopped as they came near, and crept slowly backward as he snarled at them. They charged him, stamping with their hooves until he turned to slink back into the woods with his tail between his legs. He was not going to eat a sheep today! Calm once more, Lloyd and Laverne hummed softly as they went back to their friends.

Look closely when passing by green pastures, dotted with woolly sheep. You may see llamas among them watching the lambs for their mamas.

SPIKE MAKES A FRIEND

JUST OUTSIDE of a little mountain village in the Adirondack Mountains there is a road leading farther north. It is a narrow road that has many sharp dips and hills as it winds its way to Woodgate settlement. There it turns again toward the high peaks.

In the fragrant forest that spreads on either side of this road, a small porcupine called Spike was born one spring. Even as a newborn cub, Spike had a round little face, with bright, dark eyes and a chubby body that was covered with dark hair.... tipped with sharp quills! Before long, his mother knew it was time to send him to live on his own. She told him that his quills were his defense against his enemies. "If you are in danger, point your tail and hit your enemy with your quills." She nudged him lovingly.

"But, Mama why would I do that?" Spike could not believe that anyone could be his enemy. He was a happy little fellow, who chuckled to himself as he waddled along on his short, stubby legs. For most of his day, he looked for grubs and plant shoots to eat. Who could be angry with him for that? Of course, he *did* like to chew on wood pilings that had a

nice salty taste. His mama said that came from being handled by humans. After dark, when the humans were inside, he sometimes looked for wooden tools that had been left outside, and he *did* like their taste. Even so, he did not think he had any enemies. He just wished that he had at least one friend.

After he left his mama he was very lonely. One sunny afternoon, as he sat on an old log, idly looking for grubs to eat, he heard a noise behind him. *What is that?* The loud noise scared him, and his tail shot up. His quills quivered as he slapped his tail on the log.

"Hey! Watch where you point those things!"

Spike spun around. Sitting a safe distance away was a long-eared rabbit. He sat up on his back feet and glared at Spike.

"I'm sorry." Spike apologized. "You scared me."

"I didn't mean to scare you. When I jumped over that bush I landed on a branch and it snapped." The rabbit carefully nosed a loose quill on the ground. He looked at its sharp, hooked end. "This could really hurt!"

"Mama told me it is my only defense against my enemies.... and I don't have any friends either. I get very lonely sometimes."

The rabbit looked at him thoughtfully. "I guess I could be your friend – if you promise not to hit me with those things."

"I would never do that!" Spike was so excited that he fell off the log and rolled over. When he got awkwardly to his feet, his quills were shaking again.

"Watch out!" Jack rabbit jumped back, and he kept a careful distance from Spike as they went down a path that led to the road. He told Spike which animals that they met were friendly, and which ones he should stay away from.

When they reached Jack's burrow, he explained about Spike's quills to his two brothers and his sister. Spike promised them that he would always be careful not to hit them with his tail, and they agreed to be his friends too.

That night, as the moon rode high in the sky over the forest, Spike curled up on a pile of pine branches where he had made a nest near Jack's burrow. *I have a friend – maybe two or three friends!* Happily, he closed his eyes and fell asleep.

A NEW NAME FOR BUSTER

I N THE FOREST near the little mountain village of Thendara a beautiful fawn was born just as the weather turned mild and the animals knew it was Spring again. He opened his eyes one morning when his mother lovingly licked him clean, and his ears stood up as he heard the gurgle of the Moose River where it ran close to his home.

He struggled to his feet and took his first shaky steps as he looked at the tall trees around him. For these first weeks of his life he stayed close to his mother, but as the weather grew warmer, he saw other fawns with their mothers in the forest. They wanted him to run and play with them. He was still awkward when he ran. One morning, after rain had left the ground slippery, he jumped over a log, and fell with all four legs spread out. He tried to stand up, but one of his front feet would not hold him. His mother ran to his side, and helped him limp to their den, using only three feet. For a long time he was able to hobble only on those three legs. At last his injured leg healed and he could walk again. The hoof of his injured leg had broken at its first joint, and now it laid flat against the ground when he limped along, trying to keep up with his friends.

Sometimes friends can be cruel, and when some of them started to call him "Busted," it soon became the name all of his friends used. He told himself that he didn't mind, and he joined them in games that he could never win because of his deformed foot.

By the time that summer came to Thendara, he was able to do most of the things that other deer could, only it took him much longer. He was a beautiful young buck. One day, he and two of his friends wandered into a clearing beside the river. He heard a noise, and saw that a house had been built there. A human with long blonde hair was sitting in a camp chair. His two friends gave a startled snort and ran into the woods, but Busted stood still.

The woman smiled and held out a carrot. "Oh, you are so pretty!" Her voice was soft. He edged closer, and she sat very still. He reached out and timidly nibbled at the carrot. His two friends came slowly out of the forest, and before long the human had given them each a carrot to chew.

Every day the three yearlings came back to the clearing and every day the woman fed them. His two friends leapt back into the woods to play as soon as they finished their treats, but Busted stayed to graze near his new friend. He often laid down in the shade when his foot gave him pain, and she talked softly to him when they were alone.

One afternoon, as the shadows grew long, she reached out and rubbed him between his ears. "I must give you a name!" She stroked his head. "I had a dog once when I was a little girl, and he was almost your color. His name was Buster. Would you like that name? Yes! That is what I shall call you."

Buster? I like that! He nudged her hand with his velvet nose, and she laughed.

"I think you like it! That is what I will call you." Every day she called to him when he came into her clearing. "Hello, Buster!" The sound of his new name made him happy. His friends called him that too before long. Life was good.

The weather changed quickly and winter came again to the mountains. Food became scarce, and deer wandered closer to the clearing looking for food. Every day Buster came timidly to the deck of the house, and his human friend always gave him a pan of food. While he lowered his head to eat, she talked to him, and rubbed his head. When she saw how hungry the deer were, she brought food out for all of them. Now, instead of laughing at his crippled foot, they were happy to be his friend.

ADIRONDACK FAIRY TALES II
Tell Me a Story

BARTHOLOMEW'S ADVENTURE

THERE IS A BEAUTIFUL place in the mountains called Beaver Meadows. Near it is Beaver River, and it was there that a young beaver, called Bartholomew, was born early one year while the waters of the river were still very cold.

Bartholomew's lodge was cozy and warm when he opened his dark eyes a few days after he was born. His mother had four babies. There was Bartholomew and his three sisters. His four older brothers, born the year before, still lived with them. That made eight children for Mama and Papa beaver to care for. They were busy!

His older brothers were full grown now and would find homes of their own next year. This year they helped their father, Buck, to bring food to the lodge where their mother was busy nursing her babies. Their home was in a cone-shaped pile of branches that Mama and Papa beaver had built in the river. It stuck out of the water with a hole at the top that brought air into their living room. Close to this room, there were tunnels so the busy beavers could swim

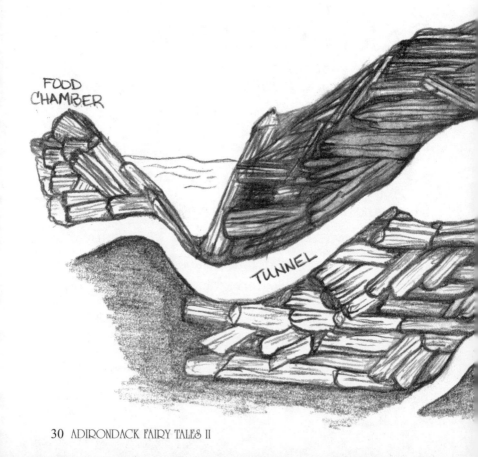

outside. Near their lodge there was another storage shed on the bottom of the river. It was made just like their lodge and held delicious willow and birch shoots that all beavers love.

Bartholomew was only a few weeks old the first time that he followed his mother out of his warm home. His dark eyes widened as he saw the long dam that stretched across the river, just a little distance from the pool where he surfaced. His busy parents and his older brothers had built the sturdy dam out of

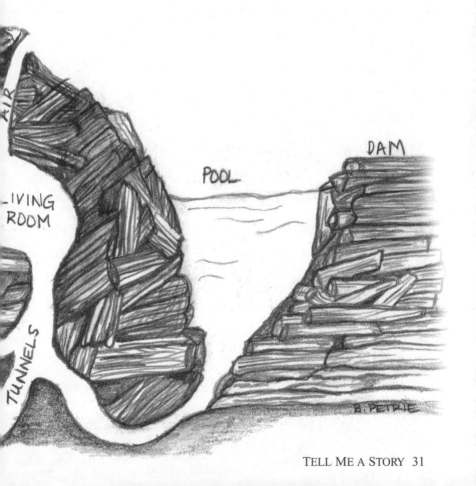

trees felled with their sharp teeth last summer. They dragged the trees to the stream, and pushed them into the water with their short, powerful front paws. Next, they filled in the dam with smaller branches and mud from the bottom of the river. Soon water poured into a pool outside of their den.

Bartholomew loved swimming and diving in this pool. His thick brown fur kept him warm and his sharp ears and eyes warned him of danger. He had a wide tail that helped to propel him through the water, and he had great fun slapping it on the water – until his mother stopped him.

"Your tail is meant to warn us of danger when you hit the water. It is not a plaything!" She scolded him.

"Sorry." Bartholomew muttered. He hated for his mother to be angry with him. He still liked to snuggle close to her, even though he could look for food himself now.

One morning, his father came hurrying into the lodge. "Quick! Come outside!" All of them swam quickly down one of the tunnels and poked their heads above the water. *Where is our dam? Where is our pool?* Bartholomew gasped as he saw that the water was so shallow that he could not dive.

Their dam was gone! The lodge was almost entirely out of the water.

"Our dam has been destroyed! The water has all gone downstream. We must leave and find a new home before it is too late." Buck urged his family down the river.

Looking around them, Bartholomew saw other beavers swimming downstream too. "Where are we going? Why can't we stay in our lodge?" Bartholomew's sister, Betsy, whined.

"Humans are destroying the dams because they keep the water back from their farms. They will destroy our lodges too." Buck led his family, and Bartholomew struggled to keep up with him. They swam for a long time. Finally, they stopped to eat and rest, but Bartholomew was too excited to stay still. He slipped under the water and swam away.

When he came up for air, he found himself in a section of the swiftly flowing water between two rows of trees standing along its edge. *Wow! I like it here! This is where we should make our new home!* He flipped onto his back and looked up at leafy branches on either side of him. *I am going to cut down a tree and stay here until Mama and Papa find me. This is just right for our new lodge!*

He climbed up on the bank and chose a tall birch tree that stood on the edge of the shore. He attacked the tree with his sharp front teeth, and he chewed eagerly, barely tasting the delicious bark in his excitement. At last, just as he was starting to feel tired, he felt the tree start to tip. He rose on his hind legs and pushed mightily. The tree fell across the water with a loud splash.

He was about to start on another tree when he saw his father and his four big brothers swimming down the river towards him. He jumped into the water and swam to meet them. "Look! I found a new place for us to live!"

His father scolded him. "You should never swim off by yourself! We thought something bad had happened to you!"

"But look," Bartholomew argued. "Isn't this great? I cut down a tree so we can start building our dam."

When he saw that he was really not hurt, Buck looked at the tree floating across the width of the river, and he nuzzled his son's head. "You are right. We will build right here…. but you must promise me that you will never leave us again. You frightened us. Here comes your mother and sisters."

Bartholomew promised. He was happy that his family was with him again, and before long they were all busy. When their new home was finished, Bartholomew was proud that he had become an important part of his family.

POKEY'S GRANDPA

A SMALL RED FOX CUB was born not too long ago near a fox run on Mount Pisgah, near Saranac Lake, high in the Adirondack mountains. His parents soon began to call him "Pokey" because he pushed his sharp nose into everything. Pokey has a pointed face, with a white tip near his black nose. His fur is a pretty orange color, and he has black legs. His bushy tail is a mixture of all of his colors, orange like his back, white like his stomach, and black like his legs and nose. The tip of his tail is white. Right now, as he came out of the fox den dragging an old faded blanket, he was holding his head high, trying to keep it out of the dirt while he looked for his mother, Henrietta.

"Pokey, where did you find that?" His mother lifted her head from the warm grassy slope of the fox run where she was enjoying the sun.

"It was way back in the corner of our den." Pokey dropped the faded, dirty cloth next to his mother. "What is it?"

His mother hesitated, and looked thoughtful. "It is time for you to hear about your great-grandfather." She gave him an affectionate lick. "Your are like him. He had a nose he was always poking into things too. Come with me."

She rose and started across the lush green slope that had been named Mount Pisgah many years before. At the edge of a clearing she stopped. Just across from them was a huge statue of a human. He was sitting in a big chair that had its front legs tipped up on a low box. He seemed to be looking out at the mountains and the lake below them. Across this human's legs was a blanket.

Pokey sat down with a thump. *It looked like his blanket!*

His mother smiled, knowing what he was thinking.

"Your grandfather stole your blanket one day when that human left it on his chair. He was a gentle man, and he was very sick when he came to the mountains. He sat outside in a chair like that every day. Being tipped back helped him to breathe."

"What happened to him?" Pokey was eager. "Did he try to take his blanket back?"

His mother frowned. "I don't think he ever knew what happened to his blanket. The mountain air made him well. He lived here all the rest of his life, just like your great-grandfather. Your great-grandfather liked this man, he was not like some other men who shot members of our family."

Pokey looked up at her as he carefully put his blanket down. "Why is his statue here?"

"His name was Doctor Edward Livingston Trudeau. When he found out that the air up here made him better, he brought other people here to cure them. For a long time there were a lot of little dens – cottages, the humans called them. People who were sick with a disease called tuberculosis, like the doctor, came and stayed until they were well." She stood up. "Come with me." They trotted across the slope to where they could see some big buildings. "These buildings are here because of this man. The humans do work inside to find cures for diseases that kill other humans."

Pokey looked over at the big buildings and was glad he didn't live too close to them. "Can I keep Grandpa's blanket?"

"Your grandfather would like that, I think. Take it back to your bed." They trotted back the way they had come. Pokey dragged the faded old blanket carefully. He put it in the corner of the den where he slept, and when he went to sleep that night he dreamed about his great grandfather.

If you should visit Saranac Lake in the Adirondack mountains you will find the statue that Pokey saw, and you can learn more about the story of that good and gentle doctor.

BANDIT SAVES THE DAY

A WINDING MOUNTAIN ROAD turns before it reaches Tupper Lake, and leads to an enchanting woodland glen.

Horseshoe Lake is home to many mountain animals. The lake's clear water holds all kinds of fish native to the mountains. Trout jump, and Bass glide through the marshy bottom. Its grassy banks provide a place for animals to make themselves a home. In the hollow of a big Oak tree that had been hit by a lightning storm, there lived a family of raccoons. The smallest of them is called "Bandit". His mother named him that when he kept stealing combs, mirrors, and other shiny things from campers who came to the lake on their vacations.

Bandit has a pointed, dark brown nose, and black hair that spreads across his eyes like a mask. His round furry body is covered with dark brown and gray fur. He has black feet and a striped brown and black bushy tail. Theirs was a happy family. His father was a good provider, and Bandit and his two sisters depended on him to bring them the food they could not seem to find for themselves. Suddenly, his father was taken away from them. Raccoons wander during the dark night, and one night Bandit's father was put up in a tree by two vicious dogs, and killed. Bandit and his family waited for him to return. The next day his mother sadly told them that he would not be coming back. "You are the one who must help me feed the family now, Bandit."

"How Mama? What can I do?" He felt helpless.

"Remember how your father showed you how he fished?" His mother nudged him gently from the nest. "You must try now by yourself."

Bandit wandered to the edge of the lake as it grew dark that afternoon. He could see fish moving through the marshy grass – and he *did* remember watching his father fish. He crouched over the edge of the water, and like his father, watched quietly until a fish came near. Then he swept his paw through the water and tossed the big fish up on the grass! He could not believe he had really done it until he heard his mother chuckle. She and his sisters were watching him!

They eagerly started to eat the fish as he turned back to the water. Before long he managed to catch two more big trout. When they returned to their den, they had full stomachs. Bandit slept soundly, proud that he had become the head of his family.

Tell Me a
Story

ROSIE FINDS
A MATE

THERE IS A WONDERFUL place in the
mountains where winding roads lead to a
small settlement. In a clearing next to Stillwater's
calm waters there is a Forest Ranger's cabin, and in
the forest which surrounds this clearing a family of
skunks live.

The weather was just starting to warm when
Rosie was born. Her pointed face had a white strip
that marked the space between her eyes and wrapped
around her small black ears. It curved down each

side of her furry black back. Her bushy white tail had a broad black stripe down its middle, and her black feet were small and dainty. Her mother was very proud of her beautiful daughter.

Each night, as the forest grew dark, Rosie's mother took her family out to look for food. Everything was so exciting! Rosie found herself releasing scent from the pouch near her back legs as she scurried around. Her mother warned her. "Humans do not like our smell. If they catch you, they will chase you away or sometimes even trap you. You must be careful to use your scent only when you are in danger."

Rosie liked her odor, but she tried to do as her mama said. As long as she stayed with her brother and sister, she was happy. The time came that summer that her brother went off to find a mate, and her sister, Lily, who really was not as pretty as Rosie, left their den to start a family of her own with a mate. Sadly, there were no other young male skunks near her den and Rosie was lonesome as the long summer was ending. Every day she rolled in a bank of flowers, hoping they would make her smell nice, but it did no good.

The ground was covered with bright red and yellow leaves, and the days grew shorter. Like most skunks, Rosie liked the dark night, and she wandered farther from her den as she looked for food. One night, as the moon rode high in the sky, she walked into the Forest Ranger's yard, where he kept a tin plate of food for hungry animals. Carefully, she crept up to the plate and settled down to chew on an ear of corn.

She heard a noise and quickly turned, releasing a little scent, as she saw a handsome skunk that she had never seen before.

"Careful now!" The other skunk chuckled. "I am hungry too. Can we share?"

Rosie lowered her eyes shyly. ***He is so handsome!*** His white stripe went straight up his sharp face, between his black ears, and down the center of his back. His tail had a white stripe in its middle, and a black fringe on either side.

"You scared me! Of course we can share." Rosie moved over so that he could stand next to her. They ate in friendly silence, but Rosie watched him from under her long lashes.

"What is your name? I am called Sam." The handsome skunk moved closer.

"I'm Rosie." She lowered her lashes again.

"Let's take a walk." Sam nudged her gently and they walked into the forest behind them. "I have been looking for a girl like you."

Rosie rubbed against him happily. She knew she had found her mate!